CLICK, CLACK, MOO
Cows That Type

For my Dad — D. C.
To Sue Dooley — B. L.

SIMON SPOTLIGHT
An imprint of Simon & Schuster Children's Publishing Division
1230 Avenue of the Americas, New York, New York 10020
This Simon Spotlight edition December 2016
Text copyright © 2000 by Doreen Cronin
Illustrations copyright © 2000 by Betsy Lewin
SIMON SPOTLIGHT, READY-TO-READ, and colophon are registered trademarks of Simon & Schuster, Inc.
For information about special discounts for bulk purchases, please contact Simon & Schuster Special Sales at
1-866-506-1949 or business@simonandschuster.com.
Manufactured in the United States of America 1116 LAK
2 4 6 8 10 9 7 5 3 1
Cataloging-in-Publication Data is available from the Library of Congress.
ISBN 978-1-4814-6541-0 (hc)
ISBN 978-1-4814-6540-3 (pbk)
ISBN 978-1-4814-6542-7 (eBook)

CLICK, CLACK, MOO
Cows That Type

by Doreen Cronin   pictures by Betsy Lewin

Ready-to-Read

Simon Spotlight

New York   London   Toronto   Sydney   New Delhi

Farmer Brown has a problem.
His cows like to type.
All day long he hears:

Click, clack, **moo.**
Click, clack, **moo.**
Clickety, clack, **moo.**

At first, he couldn't believe his ears.
Cows that type?
Impossible!

Click, clack, **moo.**
Click, clack, **moo.**
Clickety, clack, **moo.**

Then, he couldn't believe his eyes.

It was bad enough the cows had
found the old typewriter in the barn,
now they wanted electric blankets!
"No way," said Farmer Brown.
"No electric blankets."
So the cows went on strike.
They left a note on the barn door.

"No milk today!" cried Farmer Brown.
In the background, he heard the cows
busy at work:

Click, clack, **moo.**
Click, clack, **moo.**
Clickety, clack, **moo.**

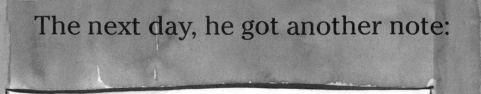

The next day, he got another note:

Dear Farmer Brown,
The hens are cold too.
They'd like electric
blankets.
Sincerely,
The Cows

The cows were growing impatient
with the farmer.
They left a new note on the barn door.

"No eggs!" cried Farmer Brown.
In the background he heard them.

Click, clack, **moo.**
Click, clack, **moo.**
Clickety, clack, **moo.**

"Cows that type. Hens on strike!
Whoever heard of such a thing?
How can I run a farm
with no milk and no eggs!"
Farmer Brown was furious.

Farmer Brown got out his
own typewriter.

> Dear Cows and Hens:
> There will be no
> electric blankets.
> You are cows and hens.
> I demand milk and eggs.
> Sincerely,
> Farmer Brown

Duck was a neutral party,
so he brought the ultimatum
to the cows.

The cows held an emergency meeting.
All the animals gathered
around the barn to snoop,
but none of them could
understand Moo.
All night long, Farmer Brown
waited for an answer.

Duck knocked on the door
early the next morning.
He handed Farmer Brown a note:

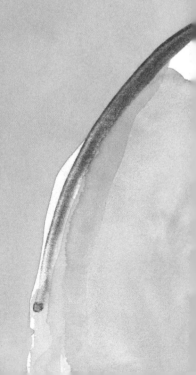

Dear Farmer Brown,
We will exchange our typewriter
for electric blankets.
Leave them outside the barn door
and we will send Duck over
with the typewriter.
Sincerely,
The Cows

Farmer Brown decided this was a good deal.

He left the blankets
next to the barn door
and waited for Duck to come
with the typewriter.

The next morning he got a note:

Dear Farmer Brown,
The pond is quite boring.
We'd like a diving board.
Sincerely,
The Ducks

Click, clack, **quack.**
Click, clack, **quack.**
Clickety, clack, **quack.**